AF228625

GIRLS' BASKETBALL

By Brendan Flynn

SportsZone

An Imprint of Abdo Publishing
abdobooks.com

abdobooks.com

Published by Abdo Publishing, a division of ABDO, PO Box 398166, Minneapolis, Minnesota 55439. Copyright © 2022 by Abdo Consulting Group, Inc. International copyrights reserved in all countries. No part of this book may be reproduced in any form without written permission from the publisher. SportsZone™ is a trademark and logo of Abdo Publishing.

Printed in the United States of America, North Mankato, Minnesota.
102021
012022

Cover Photos: Colin Edwards/Alamy, (girl); Shutterstock Images, (basketball)
Interior Photos: Nick Wass/AP Images, 4–5; Elaine Thompson/AP Images, 7, 20–21, 39; AJ Mast/AP Images, 10; Jevone Moore/Icon Sportswire/Getty Images, 12–13; Eileen T. Meslar/AP Images, 15; M. Anthony Nesmith/Icon Sportswire/AP Images, 17, 26; Aris Messinis/Getty Images Sport/Getty Images, 23; Nick Wosika/Icon Sportswire/AP Images, 25, 28–29; Rich von Biberstein/Icon Sportswire/AP Images, 32; Duncan Williams/Icon SMI/Corbis/Icon Sportswire/Getty Images, 34; Abbie Parr/Getty Images Sport/Getty Images, 36–37; Jordon Kelly/Cal Sport Media/AP Images, 42; Shutterstock Images, 44

Editor: Charlie Beattie
Series Designer: Jake Nordby

Library of Congress Control Number: 2021941592

Publisher's Cataloging-in-Publication Data

Names: Flynn, Brendan, author.
Title: Girls' Basketball / by Brendan Flynn
Description: Minneapolis, Minnesota : Abdo Publishing, 2022 | Series: Girls' SportsZone | Includes online resources and index.
Identifiers: ISBN 9781532196331 (lib. bdg.) | ISBN 9781098218140 (ebook)
Subjects: LCSH: Basketball--Juvenile literature. | Sports for girls--Juvenile literature. | Basketball for girls--Juvenile literature. | Team sports--Juvenile literature.
Classification: DDC 796.323--dc23

TABLE OF
CONTENTS

1
JUMP SHOOTING WITH
ELENA
DELLE DONNE
4

Elena Delle Donne wasn't the first option on the play. After all, she was just a rookie. And the Chicago Sky had plenty of veteran stars available to take the last shot. But even in her first year, Delle Donne had demonstrated a knack for making big plays. And with the clock ticking down in a 2013 game against the Phoenix Mercury, she did it again.

The score was tied 68–68 with 5.8 seconds left. Delle Donne took an inbound pass from teammate Epiphanny Prince near center court. The Mercury's DeWanna Bonner, one of the top defenders in the Women's National Basketball Association (WNBA), came out to guard Delle Donne.

Delle Donne took a couple of dribbles toward the basket as she looked for an open teammate. She wanted to pass the ball back to Prince, but Prince couldn't shake her defender. Time was running out, and Delle Donne knew she had to make her move.

While playing for the Washington Mystics, Elena Delle Donne, *right*, hoists a jump shot over Los Angeles Sparks defender Jantel Lavender in 2018.

She dribbled to her left, and Bonner followed her. Then Delle Donne spun back to the right, finding space to shoot just inside the free-throw line. She jumped and released the ball with 0.5 seconds remaining on the clock. The ball swished through the net as the horn sounded. The dramatic jump shot gave the Sky a 70–68 victory.

The play not only demonstrated Delle Donne's shooting skills. It also showed how much trust she had earned from her teammates so early in her career.

"The play was for [Prince]," Chicago center Sylvia Fowles said. "I'm pretty sure they knew it was going to Piph because everybody ran to Piph, but the clock was winding down and [Elena], as always, had the green light to go."

Big Shot Maya

The Minnesota Lynx won four WNBA titles between 2011 and 2017. One big factor in their success was the shooting ability of guard Maya Moore. The six-time All-Star and 2014 league MVP was one of the top five WNBA three-point shooters for six straight seasons. One of her biggest moments came in 2015. She hit a three-pointer at the buzzer to lift the Lynx past the Indiana Fever 80–77 in Game 3 of the WNBA Finals. Minnesota went on to win the title two games later.

Delle Donne generally has been given the green light to shoot wherever she's played. From her high school and college days in Delaware to her WNBA career with the Sky and later

with the Washington Mystics, the six-time All-Star has carried teams with her jump shot.

It helps that at 6 feet, 5 inches, she's tall enough to shoot over most players. And as her play against Phoenix showed, she also has the agility and ball-handling skills to create a shot for herself.

Delle Donne is a pure shooter from pretty much anywhere on the court. She won the WNBA Most Valuable Player (MVP) Award in 2015 when she averaged a career-high 23.4 points per game. She won her second MVP award in 2019 while leading Washington to its first WNBA title.

Much of Delle Donne's success is credited to her famous work ethic. She's usually the first player on the court before practice and the last one to leave after. She does this to work on her shot. But it also demonstrates a leadership quality her teammates respect. "Every single day she comes in with the same efficiency, whether she's tired, whether she's hurting, whether she's fatigued," said Natasha Cloud, Delle Donne's teammate on the Mystics. "And when you have that in your leader, it's easy to follow her example."

The Jump Shot

Making jump shots is not an easy task. Many professional players make less than 50 percent in games. But Delle Donne makes the jump shot look easy. She can rise above defenders and nail shots from all over the court. Any team that has great jump shooters like Delle Donne has an advantage.

There are other ways players can score in basketball. The layup is a common shot. Free throws are important too. Both of those shots take a lot of practice. But jump shots are the hardest to make. That is especially true for three-pointers.

The best scorers often take hundreds of practice shots between games.

The first key to a good jump shot is finding a balanced position. The player's feet and body should be square to the basket. That means her body should be directly facing the hoop. Then the player must jump upward. The goal is to release the shot while rising and at or near the highest point of the jump. This makes it harder for a defender to block the shot.

Shooting fundamentals are also key. In a jump shot, the player's off hand steadies the ball. Then the shooting hand extends upward and launches the ball toward the hoop with a flick of the wrist. The shooting hand should always follow through toward the basket for maximum accuracy. The mechanics should be the same every time.

"For me, everything is about simplicity," Delle Donne said. "So when I shoot a jump shot, I want my arm to be in the same

"50–40–90" Club

In 2019 Delle Donne became the first WNBA player to join the "50–40–90" club. That means she made at least 50 percent of her field goal attempts, 40 percent of her three-point attempts, and 90 percent of her free throws over the course of a season. It's an exclusive club. Only eight players had accomplished the same feat in the National Basketball Association (NBA) by 2021, a league that predates the WNBA by more than 40 years.

Maya Moore, *left*, of the Minnesota Lynx sets for her game-winning three-point shot in Game 3 of the 2015 WNBA Finals against the Indiana Fever.

place every single time, because in a game your feet are never going to be the same—you might be pushed off balance, you might be fading away. But if I can get my arm to a 90-degree angle, all I have to do is lift and flick, which usually puts me in a good position to make the shot."

A good jump shooter makes life harder for defenders. They always have to guard a good shooter closely. But playing defense too tight makes it easier for the offensive player to beat a defender with a dribble. In addition, good jump shooters can be more effective against zone defenses. In zones, teams pack defenders closer to the basket and guard an area, rather than an individual. That usually leaves more open space for jump shooters. Of course, the most important benefit of good jump shooting is that a player can use it from almost anywhere on the court.

QUICK TIP:
AROUND THE WORLD

Even the best players have their sweet spots. These are places on the court where they are the most comfortable—and successful—shooting the ball. It is important to be versatile, though. Life is easier for a defender if you shoot from the same spot all game. One way to practice shooting from different locations is a game called Around the World. With a partner, pick six spots on the court. One player starts by shooting from the first spot. If she makes it, she moves on to the next spot. If she misses the shot, then the other player takes over. The first person to travel "around the world" by making a shot from all six spots wins.

2

PASSING WITH
SKYLAR DIGGINS-SMITH

Crunch time is when the best players need to play their best. That's when stars like Skylar Diggins-Smith shine brightest. Diggins-Smith, a point guard for the Phoenix Mercury, put her passing skills on display late in the fourth quarter of a game against her former team, the Dallas Wings, in 2021. In the process, she showed why she is one of the top point guards in the WNBA.

With Phoenix leading by seven, Diggins-Smith took a pass on the left wing. Teammate Brittney Griner set a screen and gave Diggins-Smith room to dribble. Then Griner turned toward the basket, where Diggins-Smith found her all alone for a dunk. The textbook pick-and-roll play gave the Mercury a little more breathing room.

Less than a minute later, Diggins-Smith was dribbling at the top of the key. She saw teammate Kia Nurse cut to the basket along the baseline. Diggins-Smith threaded a perfect

Skylar Diggins-Smith of the Phoenix Mercury prepares to pass against the Los Angeles Sparks during a 2021 game.

Who's the Best?

bounce pass to Nurse, who made an easy layup.

Two possessions later, Dallas left the Mercury's Kia Vaughn open in the corner. Diggins-Smith hit her with a chest pass, and Vaughn drained the open jump shot. Diggins-Smith finished the game with 21 points and seven assists as Phoenix pulled out an 89–85 victory.

"She's a winner," Mercury coach Sandy Brondello said. "I mean she's just got this competitive nature. . . . She's just so crafty, and she loves this moment. [If we] put the ball in her hands, she's going to play defense, she's going to lead us, she's going to score. I'm just really, really proud of her."

Diggins-Smith joined the Mercury in 2020 after taking a year away from the game to give birth to her son. Her teammates knew they had just added a dynamite point guard to the roster. "She is already helping us tremendously—her [decision] making,

Courtney Vandersloot, *right*, of the Chicago Sky set a WNBA record with 258 assists in 2018. She broke it the next year when she dished out 300.

finding the open person, attacking and hitting her shots, her taking control," Griner said. "She is really going to open things up for me."

It has been a beneficial relationship for both players. Diggins-Smith and Griner helped lead the Mercury to the

Portuguese Passing Wiz

Ticha Penicheiro might be the flashiest passer ever to play in the WNBA. She became known for her behind-the-back and no-look passes to teammates. Penicheiro won college basketball's Wade Trophy in 1998 while at Old Dominion University in Norfolk, Virginia. Then she played 15 pro seasons and led the league in assists seven times. In 2008 she became the first player in the WNBA to reach 2,000 career assists.

playoffs that season. They both won a gold medal with the US Olympic team in 2021.

Passing All the Tests

Quick and effective passing is the best way to set up an offense for success. The basketball can be moved much more quickly by passing than by dribbling. An outlet pass to a teammate moving up the court can start a fast break. Passes in a half-court set can get the ball to open players or expose gaps in a defense. Plus, passing allows a team to keep all its players involved on offense. That makes it harder for defenders to focus on one star scorer or one area of the court.

Diggins-Smith has another way to be a passing threat. She can score every time she touches the ball thanks to her strong shooting ability. Defenders can't give her too much space to shoot. And if they guard her too closely, Diggins-Smith can drive to the basket. She can then decide either to shoot or to

Connecticut Sun guard Briann January delivers a chest pass during a game against the Atlanta Dream during the 2021 season.

pass the ball to players left open by defenders collapsing on her.

There are four main styles of passing. The most common is the two-handed chest pass. This is when a player passes the ball as if she is pushing it away from her body. Chest passes travel through the air. They are usually the safest way to move the ball to a teammate. However, sometimes a bounce pass works better. Having a pass bounce once off the floor can help it move through tight spaces between defenders.

Basketball players sometimes use an overhead pass. These passes are delivered by throwing the ball with two hands above the head. This pass is useful for throwing the ball over shorter opponents. It also can be used if a defender is marking the passer very tightly. The fourth type of pass, the baseball pass,

QUICK TIP:
STEP TOWARD THE TARGET

Like any good passer, Skylar Diggins-Smith usually steps toward her target when making a pass. Passing is an easy skill to practice, even if you are alone. First find a sturdy wall outside and pick a target. Then stand a few feet away from the wall and practice passing toward that target. You can do chest passes or bounce passes. Just make sure you step toward the target each time. Once you get the hang of it, start moving back after each successful pass. See if you can get back to 15 feet (4.5 m) away.

is a one-armed overhead pass. It looks just like throwing a baseball. This is useful when a player needs to move the ball a long distance.

Excellent passers such as Diggins-Smith follow certain fundamentals on chest passes. They step toward the pass receiver with one foot. This helps send the ball with force and accuracy. Following through on the passing motion also keeps passes on target. The goal is to get the ball safely to a teammate, so she is in a position to score or make another good pass.

Passing is about more than technique, though. A good passer also needs to know how to read her teammates. She knows where her teammates are at all times. She also must know where they are going. Players like Diggins-Smith often pass the ball not to a teammate but to a space where a teammate is moving.

Diggins-Smith has great technique. She also reads the game exceptionally well. Those abilities helped her finish in the top five in the league in assists three times in her first six professional seasons.

3

REBOUNDING WITH BREANNA STEWART

The Seattle Storm faced the Las Vegas Aces in Game 1 of the 2020 WNBA Finals. Breanna Stewart, Seattle's superstar forward, knew the Storm needed to be at their best. And she gave maximum effort on both ends of the court.

On defense, Stewart often found herself battling Las Vegas center Carolyn Swords underneath the basket. Swords is two inches taller and has a larger frame than the lanky 6-foot-4-inch Stewart. But Stewart showed that you don't need a size advantage to be a great rebounder.

In the first quarter, an Aces shot went off the back rim. Stewart positioned her body to keep Swords away from the ball as it came back down to the middle of the lane. Stewart then grabbed the rebound and raced down the court for a layup.

Breanna Stewart of the Seattle Storm extends to grab a rebound against the Minnesota Lynx in 2016.

Jonquel Jones

Jonquel Jones didn't play college ball at one of the premier basketball schools in the country, such as the University of Connecticut, the University of Notre Dame, or the University of South Carolina. She played at George Washington University, a school in Washington, DC. Many fans did not know much about her when she joined the WNBA in 2016. But it didn't take Jones long to make her mark on the league. In her second year, Jones set the WNBA single-season record with 403 rebounds. She averaged a league-high 11.9 per game. She did it again in 2019 at 9.7 per game. That year she made the league's All-Defensive team and played in her second WNBA All-Star Game.

Stewart used her reach to win a battle in the second quarter. Danielle Robinson of the Aces missed a driving layup, and Swords was in position for the rebound. But just as Swords was about to grab the ball off the front rim, Stewart leaped above her and took advantage of her 7-foot wingspan to swat the ball away. Stewart eventually controlled the loose ball and passed it to teammate Sue Bird. That started another fast break. Stewart hustled down the court to receive Bird's pass for a layup.

Later in the quarter, Stewart and Swords were back at it. This time, after a Las Vegas miss, Stewart used her body to pin Swords beneath the hoop long enough that Stewart could tap the rebound to a teammate.

Stewart grabs a rebound during the 2020 Olympic final against Japan.

The game ended in a 93–80 victory for the Storm. Afterward, most of the talk was about Stewart's offensive night. After all, she scored 37 points (one shy of a record for a WNBA Finals game) and hit five of eight three-pointers. But her 15 rebounds were tied for the most of any player in the WNBA playoffs that year. She helped shut down Las Vegas's offense, and Seattle set the tone for the series. The Storm won in a three-game sweep. Stewart was named the MVP of the

Playing the Angles

When Lisa Leslie was in high school, she wanted to increase her leaping ability. So she joined the volleyball and track-and-field teams. Her hard work paid off. Leslie became one of the greatest college, Olympic, and WNBA players of all time. When she retired after the 2009 season, the 6-foot-5-inch star was the WNBA's all-time rebounding leader with 3,307 rebounds. Leslie said one of the ways to be a great rebounder is to become a student of the game. "The first thing I think about is where the ball is shot from, because a lot of rebounds are just based on the angles," she once said. "A shot from the baseline will more than likely end up coming out to the other baseline. My goal is to get there or get around my opponent as much as possible."

Finals for the second time in her career.

Success is nothing new for Stewart. She won championships in high school, college (four straight at the University of Connecticut), and the WNBA. She then added Olympic gold medals in 2016 and 2021. She is also the only college player to have won three straight National Player of the Year awards and four straight Final Four Most Outstanding Player awards.

Stewart is one of the most polished all-around players in the WNBA. And rebounding is a big part of her game. She led the league in rebounds as a rookie in 2016 and was the Storm's leading rebounder in each of her first five seasons.

Sylvia Fowles of the Minnesota Lynx became the WNBA's all-time leading rebounder during the 2020 season, surpassing former teammate Rebekah Brunson.

It helps to be tall and have long arms, but there is a lot more to rebounding than size.

Grabbing Boards

Even the best basketball players miss shots. That makes rebounding an important part of the game. For the defense, a rebound changes the possession without allowing the other team to score. For the offense, a rebound keeps a possession alive. Plus, offensive rebounds often lead to easy second-chance shots right under the basket. The team that rebounds better often wins.

Jonquel Jones of the Connecticut Sun averaged over 11 rebounds per game twice in her first five WNBA seasons.

Every player on the court can and should try to grab rebounds. But forwards and centers are usually called on to rebound more. They are usually taller players and set up closer to the basket. Because Stewart is also a good outside shooter, she rarely plays close to the basket when the Storm have the ball. But she uses her height and length to block shots and dominate the defensive glass.

There are many attributes of a good rebounder. Perhaps the most important is positioning. The foundation of many rebounds is "boxing out." This is when a player positions herself facing the basket and stands between the rim and the player she is guarding. The player who is boxing out then widens her stance to get a sturdier base. By putting her arms up and flexing her knees, she can be ready to jump and get the ball when it comes off the rim or backboard.

Quickness is also important. Rebounders want to get off the floor quickly and go after the ball with both hands. Rebounding is hard work. Good rebounders anticipate where every shot could land if it misses, and they hustle to get into position when the shot goes up.

QUICK TIP:
KEEP ARMS AND HANDS UP

When Breanna Stewart gets into rebounding position, she keeps her arms and hands up. That allows her to control the ball more easily when it comes to her. Boxing out is important to gain position. But simply being in position isn't enough. It is harder to gain possession if you have to adjust your hands while the ball is falling. One way to practice this is simply by getting in the habit of keeping your arms up on defense. Even in practice, never take a play off.

4
DEFENSE
WITH
SYLVIA
FOWLES

The moment Sylvia Fowles entered the WNBA in 2008, she became one of the top defensive players in the league. She won the WNBA Defensive Player of the Year Award in 2011, 2013, and 2016, and she had been named to the WNBA All-Defensive team nine times through 2020.

Standing 6 feet, 6 inches tall, she has the size to clear out would-be rebounders and the length to swat away shot after shot. But she also has the quickness and skill to pile up steals, either by cutting into a passing lane or stripping the ball from an opponent's hands.

Fowles put all those skills on display in Game 5 of the 2017 WNBA Finals. Her Minnesota Lynx were hosting the Los Angeles Sparks. Fowles was the league's regular-season MVP in 2017. She wanted to do everything in her power to help the Lynx avenge a five-game loss to the Sparks in the 2016 finals.

Sylvia Fowles (34) of the Minnesota Lynx defends against the Seattle Storm during a game in 2018.

Fowles set the tone in the first minute. Sparks guard Chelsea Gray drove down the left side of the lane and tried to put up a short shot. Fowles dashed across the lane to cut off Gray's path to the basket. Gray was forced to put up an awkward shot that went off the side of the backboard.

In the second quarter, the Sparks' Odyssey Sims tried a pull-up jumper from about the same spot. Fowles blocked the shot, collected the loose ball, and passed it to a Lynx teammate to end the possession.

Later in the quarter, Fowles guarded Nneka Ogwumike at the top of the key. Ogwumike tried to pass the ball to a teammate under the hoop. Fowles tipped the pass, and the Lynx stole the ball.

Record-Setting Defender

Former Indiana Fever forward Tamika Catchings won the WNBA Defensive Player of the Year Award five times during her 15-year career. She's widely known as the greatest defensive player in WNBA history. "She always impacts the game down the stretch with big-time defensive plays," said Gary Kloppenburg, one of her coaches with the Fever. "[She gets] a rebound, a blocked shot, a steal. There's nobody you'd want besides her at the end of the game to be out there defensively."

In the third quarter, Fowles swatted away a driving layup attempt from the Sparks' Alana Beard. Later, Sims tried to drive down the center of the lane, but Fowles slashed over and cut her off. Then when Sims tried to pass to a teammate in the corner, Fowles cut back and intercepted the pass.

Fowles saved her best for the fourth quarter as the Sparks tried to rally from a 10-point deficit. First, Candace Parker, the Sparks' star center, grabbed a loose ball and drove to the hoop, but Fowles swatted the shot. Fowles then rebounded missed shots on the Sparks' next three possessions.

Finally, with the Lynx up by just five with 21 seconds to play, Sims missed a three-point attempt. Fowles grabbed the rebound. It was her twentieth of the night, a record for a WNBA Finals game. After being fouled, she made both free throws to send the Lynx to an 85–76 victory. Fowles finished the game with 17 points, 20 rebounds, two steals, and three blocked shots. She was named MVP of the Finals, as the Lynx won their fourth WNBA title in seven years. "If I didn't

Defense Produces Offense

Candace Parker is one of the WNBA's most exciting offensive players. But the 6-foot-4-inch All-Star and two-time Olympic gold medalist also was the league's Defensive Player of the Year in 2020. Parker says playing strong defense leads to offensive opportunities. A steal or block can lead to a fast break against a defense scrambling to get back. "When I play defense, it gives me an advantage because I'm in the open court," she said. "So it's a win-win situation."

Fowles, *right*, blocks a shot attempt from Atlanta Dream forward Monique Billings during a 2019 game.

do anything else, I just wanted to make it my business to make sure I just go out there and rebound," Fowles said after her record-setting performance.

Defense Is Key

Many of the most successful teams stress defense as a path to championships. A team's shooting may go cold. Or they might have trouble rebounding against a taller team. But defensive effort is something a team can give during every game. That became the case as soon as Fowles joined the Lynx in 2015.

"She understands how to use her physical gifts to not just be good, but dominant," Lynx coach Cheryl Reeve said. "As far as a physical, low-block presence, I don't know that anyone in

QUICK TIP:
DEFENSE STARTS WITH STANCE

Defense starts with a well-balanced stance. Your weight should be slightly forward on the balls of your feet, and your knees should be flexed. Your head should be up for good vision. Your hands should be ready to challenge a pass, a dribble, or a shot. While defending, your hand should be up high on the ball side of the ball handler to guard a pass. The other hand should be down low on the non-ball side to protect against a cross-over dribble. With your feet just a bit wider than your shoulders, you can quickly move from side to side.

Tamika Catchings of the Indiana Fever retired after the 2016 season as the WNBA's all-time steals leader, with 1,074.

our game has been better. Syl is a combination of aggression and ability; it's impressive to be around that every day."

A team playing strong defense can count on several benefits. Good defense can force the other team to take low-percentage shots. It also can force a team to make mistakes. Bad passes and turnovers can lead to easy baskets at the other end. Good defense can take a team out of its offensive rhythm. That forces the offense to work extra hard for scoring opportunities, which can tire a team out.

There are two main defensive systems. One is man-to-man. This is when every player guards an opponent. When playing man-to-man, a player guards a single opponent for an entire possession. In zone defense, players are responsible for guarding an area of the court. The goal of zone defense is often to try to limit an opponent's close, easy shots. No matter what system a team uses, the traits that produce good defensive players and a strong team defense are similar.

Defensive players must always hustle and be responsible for their player or area. They must challenge players with the ball. They must be quick, use good footwork, and anticipate passes and shots. With strong fundamentals and desire, anyone can be a difference-maker every game, like Fowles. Reeve summed up the importance of Fowles's defensive skills simply, saying, "Sylvia Fowles is just really hard to play against."

5

BALL HANDLING WITH SUE BIRD

The Seattle Storm rolled to the 2020 WNBA title, winning all six of their playoff games. Seattle's young superstar forward, Breanna Stewart, got most of the attention for her dominant performance. But she had plenty of help from point guard Sue Bird.

Bird was just days away from turning 40 when the Finals began, but she was still one of the WNBA's best players. The Las Vegas Aces were unable to stop her. The league's all-time assist leader set a WNBA Finals record with 16 assists in Game 1. She also put her legendary ball handling skills on display.

In the second quarter, Bird brought the ball up the left side of the court. Stewart set a screen and gave Bird some space. Bird dribbled toward the corner, cut around Las Vegas center Carolyn Swords, and raced along the baseline. As a defender closed in, Bird ducked below the hoop and hit a reverse layup.

Sue Bird of the Seattle Storm surveys the court while dribbling against the Indiana Fever during a 2021 game.

Bird can use her dribbling to get free for a shot. But mostly she uses it to set up her teammates. In the fourth quarter of Game 1, she and Stewart worked a perfect pick-and-roll play. Bird dribbled around Stewart's screen, moved past a second defender, and hit Stewart with a pass for an easy layup.

In Game 2, Las Vegas led in the third quarter. But Bird went to work. Bringing the ball up the court, she hesitated briefly to freeze her defender before blowing past. Then she split two other defenders as she drove to the hoop for a basket. Seattle went on to win the game.

In the second half of Game 3, Bird's ball handling skills helped the Storm finish off the series. First, she dribbled around a screen and found room near the top of the

A "T-Spoon" of Learning

Teresa Weatherspoon might have been the best point guard of her era. She starred at Louisiana Tech University from 1984 to 1988, then in the WNBA, and on the US Olympic team. The 5-foot-8-inch guard nicknamed T-Spoon was an outstanding dribbler. She was also the league's all-time assist leader when she retired in 2004.

Weatherspoon once said that she learned to dribble as a four-year-old in Texas, playing on "a bumpy patch of dirt and grass." Learning how to control the basketball on such an uneven surface turned her into one of the world's most skilled ball handlers.

Bird makes a move against the New York Liberty during a 2018 game. Through the 2020 season, Bird had led the Storm to four WNBA titles.

three-point arc. She then used a step-back dribble and created space to drain a long jump shot.

Three minutes later, Bird found herself in a similar spot. This time, she dribbled toward the hoop. When the defense collapsed on her in the lane, she flicked a pass to teammate Jewell Lloyd in the corner. Lloyd hit a three-pointer, and the

It's in the Gloves

In 2011 Becky Hammon became just the seventh player in WNBA history to score 5,000 points. A big part of her scoring ability came from her skills as a ball handler. In 2007 the 5-foot-6-inch guard won the league's skills contest called "Dribble, Dish, and Swish."

She scored many baskets off drives that involved dribbling past defenders through the crowded lane. Hammon said one thing she did through the years to sharpen her skills was wear thick gardening gloves during dribbling drills.

Hammon was hired as an assistant coach by the NBA's San Antonio Spurs in 2014, leading to predictions that she would someday be the first female head coach in NBA history.

Storm were on their way to a 33-point blowout win.

Winning was not unusual for Bird, who won two national titles at the University of Connecticut. She also has five Olympic gold medals, and the 2020 WNBA title was her fourth with the Storm.

While at Connecticut, Bird won the Nancy Lieberman Award three times. It is given to the best point guard in college basketball based on floor leadership, playmaking, and ball handling skills. Her head coach at Connecticut, Geno Auriemma, wasn't surprised that Bird was still winning titles and making Olympic teams at age 40.

"For Sue, her incredible consistency as a player comes from her consistency as a person," said Auriemma, who was also her coach at the Olympics. "Each year she's added something that's made her more consistent, kept her healthier. There's some injuries that have happened that you can't control. But she's an incredible leader on the basketball court of epic proportions, because she understands this is what has to be done with this particular team in order to win."

Handled with Care

Few can control a basketball as well as Bird. But dribbling is one of the most important fundamental skills that all players must know. Teamwork is the key to a good and balanced offense. Yet there are many times when one player must be

QUICK TIP:
ATTACK THE CONE ZONE

Good dribbling skills such as Sue Bird's can be improved through drills and practice. One popular drill involves setting up two lines of cones on the court, with each cone 5 feet (1.5 m) from the next in a straight line. Find a partner and race each other through the cones by dribbling through them, first up and then back. Try to keep your head up while switching the ball from your right hand to your left hand. Always keep your body between the cone and the ball. This will improve speed and the ability to dribble with either hand.

While playing in a 2018 game for the Dallas Wings, Skylar Diggins-Smith uses her body to shield the ball from a Los Angeles Sparks defender.

in control of the ball. Sometimes it is the point guard bringing the ball up the court. Other times it is another player taking on a defender one-on-one. Every player needs to be able to move with the ball while also protecting it from defenders.

Good ball handlers usually control the ball with their fingers rather than the palms of their hands. They can dribble with either hand, and they can move quickly. They can also keep their eyes up to see their teammates and opponents. They can dribble just as well to both sides. They also can pass and make layups with either hand. When a player can use both hands well, she can always keep her body between the ball and her opponent.

Good ball handling skills prevent turnovers. They also allow a team to move the ball quickly around the court to find openings in a defense.

Many times during her career, Bird was able to dribble through multiple defenders while switching hands and directions. Then she could skillfully pass the ball to an open teammate or take an open shot. Ball handling skills are acquired through years of drills and practice. Players who master those skills are the hardest players to stop. "She can score, pass, and handle the ball, and she can lead," former Storm coach Lin Dunn said of Bird. "Her presence on the floor makes everyone better."

COURT DIAGRAM

BASELINE AND SIDELINE
These lines mark the borders of the court.

DIVISION LINE
This line separates the court in half. Once the offense has possession on the opponent's side of the court, it must stay on that side.

CENTER CIRCLE
The tipoff takes place here. Only the two players taking the tipoff can be inside the circle.

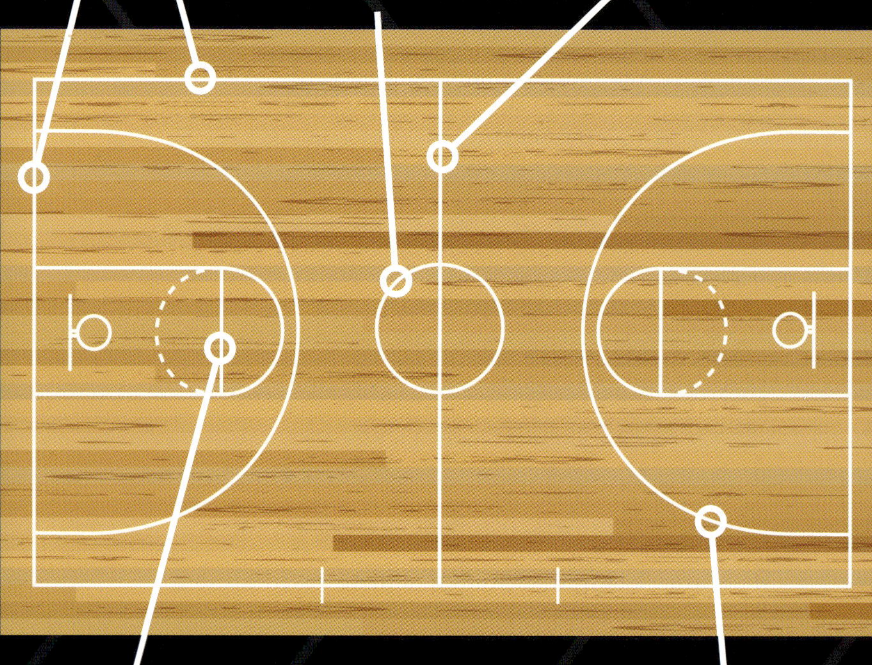

FREE-THROW LINE
A player must stand behind this line, which is 15 feet (4.6 m) from the backboard, while taking free throws.

THREE-POINT LINE
Shots made from beyond this arc are worth three points.

GLOSSARY

assist
A pass that leads directly to a basket.

avenge
To seek revenge for a previous defeat.

defender
A player from the team without the ball trying to guard or stop a player from a team with the ball.

fast break
Moving the ball up the floor quickly.

field goal
Any basketball shot that isn't a free throw.

key
The free-throw lane and the free-throw circle together.

layup
A shot made from close to the basket; an easy shot.

rebound
To catch the ball after a shot has been missed.

screen
When an offensive player legally blocks the path of a defender to open up a teammate for a shot or a pass.

steal
To take the ball from a player on the other team.

turnover
Losing the ball to the other team because of a mistake.

MORE INFORMATION

BOOKS

Carothers, Thomas. *Geno Auriemma and the Connecticut Huskies*. Minneapolis, MN: Abdo, 2019.

Sheridan, Chris. *Innovations in Basketball*. Minneapolis, MN: Abdo, 2022.

Smibert, Angie. *STEM in Basketball*. Minneapolis, MN: Abdo, 2018.

ONLINE RESOURCES

To learn more about women's basketball, please visit **abdobooklinks.com** or scan this QR code. These links are routinely monitored and updated to provide the most current information available.

PLACES TO
VISIT

Naismith Memorial Basketball Hall of Fame

1000 Hall of Fame Ave.
Springfield, MA 01105
877-4HOOPLA
hoophall.com

Opened in 1968, this museum has exhibits about the sport's birth and development and has enshrined coaches and players from men's and women's college, professional, and international teams.

Women's Basketball Hall of Fame

700 Hall of Fame Dr.
Knoxville, TN 37915
865-633-9000
wbhof.com

This facility was opened in 1999 and specifically honors the best players and coaches in the women's game. Over 170 people have been inducted.

INDEX

ABOUT THE AUTHOR

Brendan Flynn is a San Francisco resident and an author of numerous children's books.